The Tale of
Benjamin Bunny

The Tale of Benjamin Bunny

by Beatrix Potter

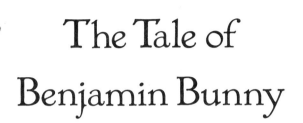

DERRYDALE BOOKS
New York • Avenel

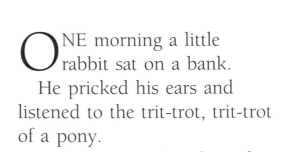

ONE morning a little rabbit sat on a bank.

He pricked his ears and listened to the trit-trot, trit-trot of a pony.

A gig was coming along the road; it was driven by Mr. McGregor, and beside him sat Mrs. McGregor in her best bonnet.

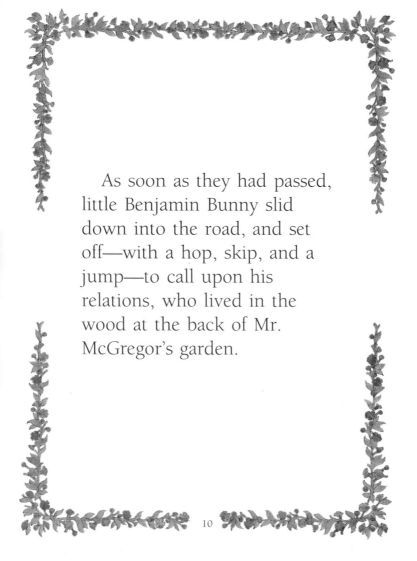

As soon as they had passed, little Benjamin Bunny slid down into the road, and set off—with a hop, skip, and a jump—to call upon his relations, who lived in the wood at the back of Mr. McGregor's garden.

That wood was full of rabbit holes; and in the neatest, sandiest hole of all lived Benjamin's aunt and his cousins—Flopsy, Mopsy, Cottontail, and Peter.

Old Mrs. Rabbit was a widow; she earned her living by knitting rabbit-wool mittens and mufflers (I once bought a set at a bazaar). She also sold herbs, and rosemary tea, and rabbit tobacco (which is what we call lavender).

Little Benjamin did not very much want to see his Aunt.

He came round the back of the fir tree, and nearly tumbled upon the top of his Cousin Peter.

Peter was sitting by himself. He looked poorly, and was dressed in a red cotton pocket handkerchief.

"Peter," said little Benjamin, in a whisper, "who has got your clothes?"

Peter replied, "The scarecrow in Mr. McGregor's garden," and described how he had been chased about the garden, and had dropped his shoes and coat.

Little Benjamin sat down beside his cousin and assured him that Mr. McGregor had gone out in a gig, and Mrs. McGregor also; and certainly for the day, because she was wearing her best bonnet.

Peter said he hoped that it would rain.

At this point old Mrs. Rabbit's voice was heard inside the rabbit hole, calling: "Cottontail! Cottontail! Fetch some more camomile!"

Peter said he thought he might feel better if he went for a walk.

They went away hand in hand, and got up on the flat top of the wall at the bottom of the wood. From here they looked down into Mr. McGregor's garden. Peter's coat and shoes were plainly to be seen upon the scarecrow, topped with an old tam-o'-shanter of Mr. McGregor's.

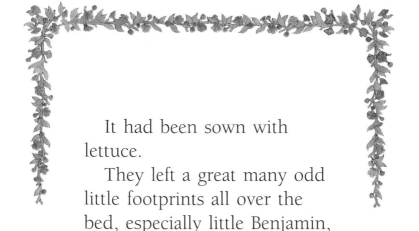

It had been sown with lettuce.

They left a great many odd little footprints all over the bed, especially little Benjamin, who was wearing clogs.

Little Benjamin said that the first thing to be done was to get back Peter's clothes, in order that they might be able to use the pocket handkerchief.

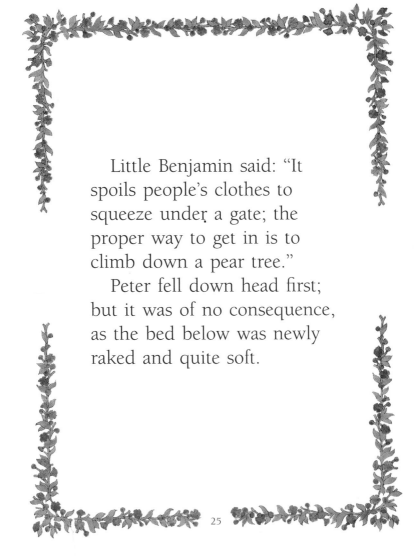

Little Benjamin said: "It spoils people's clothes to squeeze under a gate; the proper way to get in is to climb down a pear tree."

Peter fell down head first; but it was of no consequence, as the bed below was newly raked and quite soft.

Benjamin, on the contrary, was perfectly at home, and ate a lettuce leaf. He said that he was in the habit of coming to the garden with his father to get lettuce for their Sunday dinner.

(The name of little Benjamin's papa was old Mr. Benjamin Bunny.)

The lettuce certainly was very fine.

Peter did not eat anything;
he said he should like to go
home. Presently he dropped
half the onions.

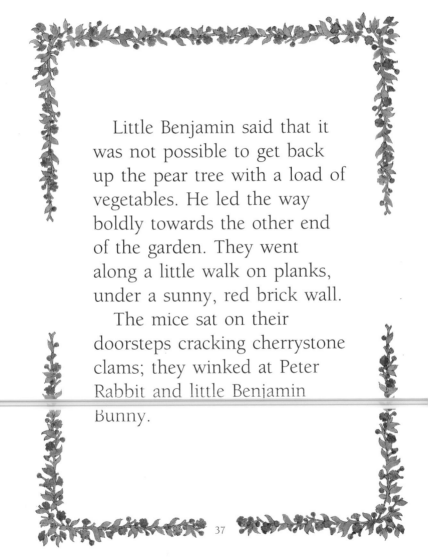

Little Benjamin said that it was not possible to get back up the pear tree with a load of vegetables. He led the way boldly towards the other end of the garden. They went along a little walk on planks, under a sunny, red brick wall.

The mice sat on their doorsteps cracking cherrystone clams; they winked at Peter Rabbit and little Benjamin Bunny.

Presently Peter let the
pocket handkerchief go again.

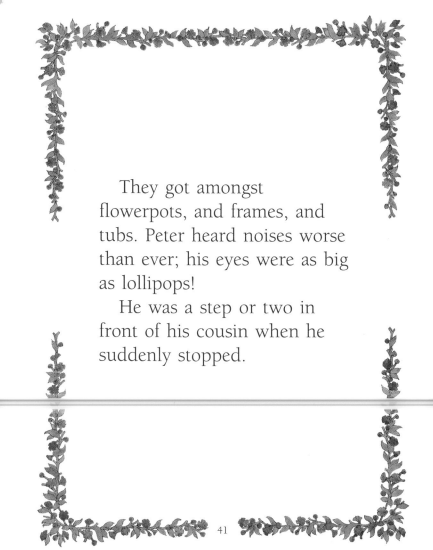

They got amongst
flowerpots, and frames, and
tubs. Peter heard noises worse
than ever; his eyes were as big
as lollipops!

He was a step or two in
front of his cousin when he
suddenly stopped.

This is what those little
rabbits saw round that corner!

Little Benjamin took one
look, and then, in half a
minute less than no time, he
hid himself and Peter and the
onions underneath a large
basket. . . .

The cat got up and
stretched herself, and came
and sniffed at the basket.

Perhaps she liked the smell
of onions!

Anyway, she sat down upon
the top of the basket.

She sat there for *five hours*.

* * * * * * * *

I cannot draw you a picture
of Peter and Benjamin
underneath the basket,
because it was quite dark, and
because the smell of onions
was fearful; it made Peter
Rabbit and little Benjamin cry.

The sun got round behind
the wood, and it was quite
late in the afternoon; but still
the cat sat upon the basket.

At length there was a pitter-
patter, pitter-patter, and some
bits of mortar fell from the
wall above.

The cat looked up and saw
old Mr. Benjamin Bunny
prancing along the top of the
wall of the upper terrace.

He was smoking a pipe of
rabbit-tobacco, and had a little
switch in his hand.

Old Mr. Bunny had no respect whatever for cats. He took a tremendous jump off the top of the wall on to the top of the cat, and cuffed it off the basket, and kicked it into the greenhouse, scratching off a handful of fur.

The cat was too much surprised to scratch back.

When old Mr. Bunny had driven the cat into the greenhouse, he locked the door.

Then he came back to the basket and took out his son Benjamin by the ears, and whipped him with the little switch.

Then he took out his nephew Peter.

Then he took out the
handkerchief of onions, and
marched out of the garden.

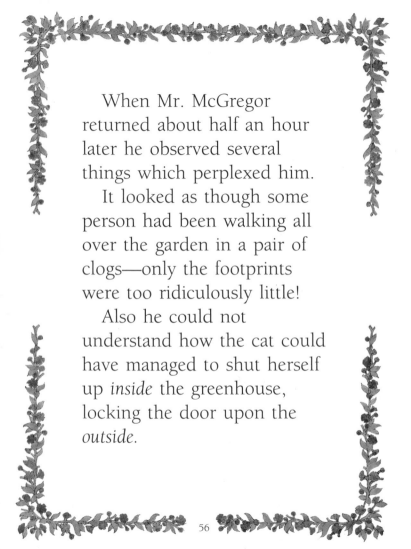

When Mr. McGregor returned about half an hour later he observed several things which perplexed him.

It looked as though some person had been walking all over the garden in a pair of clogs—only the footprints were too ridiculously little!

Also he could not understand how the cat could have managed to shut herself up *inside* the greenhouse, locking the door upon the *outside*.

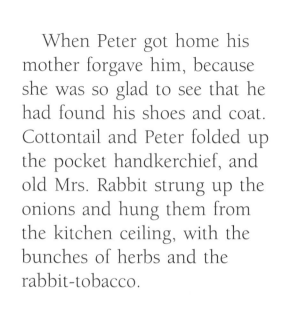

When Peter got home his mother forgave him, because she was so glad to see that he had found his shoes and coat. Cottontail and Peter folded up the pocket handkerchief, and old Mrs. Rabbit strung up the onions and hung them from the kitchen ceiling, with the bunches of herbs and the rabbit-tobacco.

THE END

ABOUT BEATRIX POTTER

Born in London in 1866, Beatrix Potter spent a lonely childhood. Her well-to-do parents did not send her to school, but instead had her taught by governesses at home. Her only friend was her younger brother Bertram. On vacations in Scotland, she and Bertram escaped into a world of farms, woods, and fields, where they delighted in watching and collecting plants, animals, and insects.

In London, yearning for the country, and the fascinating little animals she loved, Beatrix kept small pets in her nursery—a rabbit, some mice, snails, and even a hedgehog—and began to draw them, as well as plants and flowers she had seen in the countryside.

Out of these drawings grew her illustrated stories about rabbits and other small animals. They began as letters to children, then became published books. The stories were so popular that at the age of thirty-six, Beatrix Potter found herself a successful children's author. She continued to write and illustrate her delightful tales, eventually more than two dozen, and successive generations of children have cherished them.

Editorial Note

The language of Beatrix Potter's stories includes certain British words or phrases which may be unfamiliar to today's American children. Therefore, in a few cases, the text has been altered slightly to make it more comprehensible. The changes, however, have been kept to a minimum to retain the charm of the original.

Dedication

FOR THE CHILDREN OF SAWREY
FROM OLD MR. BUNNY

This 1992 edition is published by Derrydale Books, distributed by
Outlet Book Company, Inc., a Random House Company,
225 Park Avenue South, New York, New York 10003.

Printed and bound in the United States of America

Library of Congress Cataloging-in-Publication Data

Potter, Beatrix, 1866–1943.
The tale of Benjamin Bunny / by Beatrix Potter.
    p.   cm.
Summary: Peter's mischievous cousin, Benjamin Bunny, persuades
him to go back to Mr. McGregor's garden to retrieve the clothes he lost
there.
    ISBN 0–517–07240–8
    [1. Rabbits—Fiction.]   I. Title.
[PZ7.P85Tak   1992]
[E]—dc20   91–35115
                                                                        CIP
                                                                         AC

For this edition of The Tale of Benjamin Bunny:
Cover and interior design: Clair Moritz
Production supervision: Helen Marra and Ellen Reed
Editorial supervision: Claire Booss

8   7   6   5   4   3   2

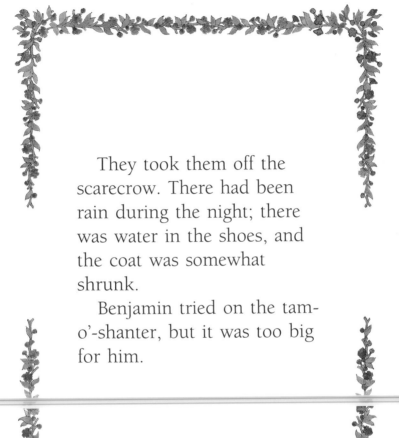

They took them off the
scarecrow. There had been
rain during the night; there
was water in the shoes, and
the coat was somewhat
shrunk.

Benjamin tried on the tam-
o'-shanter, but it was too big
for him.

Then he suggested that they should fill the pocket handkerchief with onions, as a little present for his Aunt.

Peter did not seem to be enjoying himself; he kept hearing noises.